Disney's

DOUG
Created by
Jim Jinkins

CHRONICLES

Skeeter Loves Patti?

by Jeffrey Nodelman

Illustrated by
Matthew C. Peters, Jeffrey Nodelman, Vinh Truong
and Brian Donnelly

Skeeter Loves Patti? is hand-illustrated by the same
Grade A Quality Jumbo artists who bring you
Disney's Doug, the television series.

New York

Original characters for "The Funnies" developed by Jim Jinkins and
Joe Aaron.

Copyright © 1999 by Disney Enterprises, Inc.

Printed in the United States of America.

1 3 5 7 9 10 8 6 4 2

The artwork for this book is prepared using watercolor.

The text for this book is set in 18-point New Century Schoolbook.

Library of Congress Catalog Card Number: 98-60526

ISBN:0-7868-4322-5

For more Disney Press fun, visit www.disneybooks.com

Skeeter Loves Patti?

CHAPTER ONE

"Man, am I getting tired," sighed Skeeter. "How many times can a salad spin around, anyway?"

"Just one more chorus, Skeet," replied Doug.

From the lighting booth, Doug Funnie had a perfect view of the love of his life, Patti Mayonnaise.

Doug was running the spotlight while his best friend, Skeeter, manned the lighting board for Bluffington Community Theater's upcoming music-and-dance extravaganza, *A Tale of Two Salads*, a musical poem written by Silas Bluff. Patti played the leading lady, Ava Cado. Guy Graham played her leading man, Dash Radish. Every night Doug watched as Guy and Patti danced across the stage, while Doug dreamed that he would be the one who rescued Patti from the evil clutches of Black Beet and the Beetsie Boys (played fiendishly by Roger Klotz and his gang). But

Doug was stuck watching from above.

"Snap to, little brother. You missed your last two cues. Can't you do anything right?" Judy snapped as she stuck her head into the lighting booth. "It's bad enough that you ruined our audition to perform in the show, but now you can't even run a silly spotlight! I never should have auditioned with you!"

"I never wanted to audition with you, either!" Doug shouted after Judy. "It wasn't my fault that Skeeter pulled that lighting cord across the stage."

"I couldn't help bumping Judy

off the stage and into Ms. Mimi's lap," said Skeeter. "So she didn't get a part and has to be the stage manager. At least Ms. Mimi doesn't call *her* the 'Klutzy One.'"

Doug headed for the spotlight. Right then, Skeeter dropped his cue sheets and scooted out of his chair to pick them up. Doug, not realizing that Skeeter was behind him, tripped over Skeeter. As he fell, Doug grabbed the master light switch and the stage went black.

"Hey, who killed the lights?" shouted Guy. "I can't see a—AHHHHHH!" *CRASH!*

"Oops!" Doug flipped the switch

back on. "Oh, no!" Doug cried as he surveyed the damage. Guy lay in the orchestra pit covered in sheet music, his right foot stuck

in the tuba and a bass drum wrapped around his midsection. Crowning his head was a cymbal.

"Ow!" cried Guy. "My ankle!"

"Oh, man!" cried Skeeter. "Somebody call 9-1-1!"

Although the paramedics thought that Guy's ankle was only sprained, it became obvious that Guy would not be able to dance. Doug's eyes met Ms. Mimi's.

"You . . . you over there," said Ms. Mimi, pointing toward Doug. "You will be my next star!"

"Who, me?" beamed Doug.

"No, not you. I want the Klutzy

One. The one behind you. The honking one."

"Me, honk, honk?" honked Skeeter. "Your next star? Cool, man!"

"Come with me." And she whisked Skeeter away.

CHAPTER TWO

The next day, Doug watched
Skeeter trip across the stage with
Patti. Literally.

"No, no, no!" bellowed Ms. Mimi
at Skeeter. "Get up and try again.
It's a good thing that boy's shaped
like a radish," she murmured to
herself, "or I'd have to replace him."

"Oh, Dougie!" Judy called. "I've got some help for you! Come on up, Skunky!"

"Skunky? Did you say Skunky? Not Skunky Beaumont?" Doug whispered. "Judy, Skunky can't possibly work up here. He's probably never seen a lighting booth before."

"Well," Judy retorted, "we all have to start somewhere."

"Judy, you can't . . ."

"Listen, little brother, you've caused me enough trouble! I asked Skunky if he wanted the job. He said, 'Gnarly!' That was good enough for me. Besides, nobody else would do it. This is all your fault anyway, so make the best of it. Come on up, Skunky."

"Whoa, Doug," Skunky said. "Buttons. Wires . . . and . . . whoa."

Doug sighed.

Doug caught up with Skeeter after rehearsal. "Hey, Skeet! Rough rehearsal, huh?"

"Yeah. I was dancing like a sack of potatoes. Good thing tomorrow's our day off."

"Yeah. Hey, wanna come over to my house for a while? We can watch Smash Adams videos and order a banana pizza . . . my treat. What do you say?"

"Oh . . . ah . . . yeah . . . well, I'd like to but I've got to go home and . . . wash my . . . dog."

"Wash your dog? When did you get a dog?"

"Dog? Silly me. Did I say dog? I

meant *hog*. New . . . uh . . . pet. Oh, well, gotta run. See ya, honk, honk!" And with that, Skeeter disappeared down the street.

Doug stood puzzled for a moment. "Hog?"

CHAPTER THREE

Dear Journal,
It's really been strange
lately, with Guy leaving the
cast and Skeeter taking his
place. Boy, Skeeter has all
the luck. He gets to dance
with Patti while I'm stuck
in the lighting booth with
Skunky.

"Well, Porkchop," Doug said, closing his journal and heading for the phone. "Wanna call Skeeter and see if he wants to come over for a while?" Porkchop yipped a "yes" as Doug began dialing.

"Hey, Skeet!"

"Hey, Doug, what's shakin'?" Skeeter answered.

"Aw, nothing, man. Are you doing anything?"

"Well . . . I'm not sure . . . Why do you ask?"

"Wanna come over and chow down on some popcorn?"

"Sorry, Doug. I . . . uh . . . can't."

"Why not?" questioned Doug, a little surprised.

"See, well, I . . . ah . . . have a sick . . . toe," stammered Skeeter.

"A sick toe? What happened, did your *hog* step on it?"

"No, I . . . ah . . . well, yes. Exactly. My hog stepped on it, that's it! And it got . . . sick. I can't walk on it."

"Fine. I'll come over there."

"Ah . . . no. I'm . . . still contagious. You'd get sick. Swine flu."

"Let me get this straight, Skeet," said Doug. "Your new pet hog stepped on your toe."

"Right."

"And your toe got sick."

"Right. Swine flu. Very contagious."

"Right. And that's why I can't come over."

"Right, Doug. Sorry."

"Skeeter?"

"Yes, Doug?"

"I can't wait to meet your new hog."

"His name is Spot."

"Spot?"

"Spot."

"See you later, Skeeter."

"Yeah, see ya, honk, honk." Skeeter hung up the phone.

Sick toe? Swine flu? A hog named Spot? Doug was confused when he hung up the phone.

CHAPTER FOUR

"Porkchop," Doug asked, "does Skeeter seem to be acting a little . . . weird?" Porkchop nodded yes.

Their feet draped over the back of the sofa and their heads hanging off the seat, Doug and Porkchop tried to figure why

Skeeter was acting so strange.
"What is Skeeter up to? This bugs
me, Porkchop."

"Feeling a little down, Douglas?"

Doug opened his eyes and saw
his father, Phil Funnie.

"Yeah . . . I guess so."

"You feel like talking about it?"

"Not really, Dad. Thanks anyway."

"Well, then, why don't you go outside and take a walk in the sunshine. A little fresh air always helps me feel better."

"Yeah, that's a good idea. Thanks, Dad. Come on, Porkchop. Let's play catch in the park for a while. Just the two of us." Porkchop barked his approval and they bounded out the door for Lucky Duck Park.

CHAPTER FIVE

"Here, boy," shouted Doug. "Catch!"

Barking "Tah-dah!" Porkchop completed a double backflip and caught the ball.

"I bet Skeeter has a good reason for acting so weird. I just hope it's not something really bad."

At once Doug's imagination took

off. Skeeter limped up to him, assisted with a cane and bandaged from head to toe.

"Doug," said Skeeter, "I didn't want to worry you with this, but I've only got three minutes until . . . the end."

"Oh, no!" cried Doug. "Skeeter, what's wrong?"

"Dutch elm disease, Doug."

"Dutch elm disease? Isn't that a tree disease?"

"Yeah. I'm part tree. Turns out Great Grandma Valentine married an elm."

"Skeeter, why didn't you tell me sooner?"

"Because I knew you'd . . . Doug,

there's something I have to tell you, and there's not much time left."

"What is it, Skeeter?"

"Doug, the reason I have been acting so strangely lately is that . . . that . . . TIMBER!"

"Skeeter? Skeeter? Oh, no, it's too late! Now I'll never know!"

Doug was so involved in his daydream that he did not notice the beetball until it whizzed by, bringing him back to reality. Nah, it can't be that bad, Doug thought. I mean, I think I'd know if he had a tree disease. I wonder what is going on, though.

"Okay, Porkchop, see if you can catch this one."

Doug hurled the ball so high that it went into the bushes nearby.

"Go get it, Porkchop," Doug called, watching him chase after the ball.

"I'd better go help him find that ball," Doug said, following him through the bushes a minute later.

"Porkchop, why aren't you . . ." Suddenly, Doug saw why

Porkchop hadn't returned. Doug could hardly move.

"Do you see what I see? Skeeter and Patti! And Skeeter is holding Patti's hand! Quick, let's get out of here." Not knowing what else to do, Doug headed for home.

"Sick toe, my foot!" Doug muttered under his breath.

CHAPTER SIX

Doug quietly raced up to his room to be alone with his only *real* best friend.

"Can you *believe* that?" Doug exclaimed, plopping down on his bed. Porkchop, shaking his head, let out a slight moan.

"How could Skeeter do this?

He's supposed to be my best human friend! Best friends don't steal girls from each other . . . it's the rule! *That's* why he's been avoiding me. *That's* why he's been acting so weird. No wonder he suddenly has this pet hog named Spot! It all makes sense now.

"Oh, no! Porkchop, think of all the secrets I've told him! All the things I ever said about Patti. All the doofy things I did and messes I made! I kept them hidden from her all this time, but Skeeter knows everything! What if he tells her?"

Doug immediately dove into a horrible daydream, imagining

Skeeter and Patti dressed up,
seated at a fancy restaurant.
Doug was their waiter.

"So Doug fell and turned off all the lights?" Patti laughed.

"Right," confirmed Skeeter.

"And that's how Guy hurt his ankle?"

"Right."

"And that's how we . . ."

"Yes. If Doug weren't so klutzy, we wouldn't be . . ."

"Oh, Skeeter," Patti laughed. "That Funnie boy is so . . . funny!"

"Oh, that's nothing, my dear. Wait until you hear this. His middle name is . . ."

"Oh, no!" Doug shouted in his head. "He's going to tell her my middle name is Yancey! I've got to stop him!" Doug sprinted to the table and blurted out, "Can I get you anything? Coffee, tea, me—I mean, milk?"

"That will be all, *Yancey*." Skeeter laughed as he and Patti got up to leave. Skeeter had done it.

"Just wait until I tell you about the time he wrote a poem about you and turned it in to Ms. Kristal by mistake! Then he tried . . ."

"No, Skeeter! Not that one!" shouted Doug. "I've got to stop him before he ruins my whole life!" Doug sprinted across the restaurant, tripped over a serving cart, and fell on his face at their feet.

"Very interesting doormats they have here," Skeeter said as he and Patti wiped their feet off on

Doug's back and left the restaurant laughing, arm in arm.

"Doug, time for supper. Hurry or you'll be late for your rehearsal," Doug's mother called from the kitchen.

"Oh–h–h–h!" Doug moaned. "How can I ever face them? I'm so humiliated! I can't go to the theater! Porkchop, what am I going to do?"

Porkchop jumped up on the bed next to Doug, whined, and licked his face.

"At least I've still got you, man."

CHAPTER SEVEN

"Back to rehearsal," moaned Doug. "I think I'd rather have my teeth pulled without novocaine. I'd better get there early. If I don't, I'll be sure to run into Skeeter or Patti."

When Doug got to the theater, he stealthily made his way up to the lighting booth.

As Doug watched Skeeter and Patti rehearse, he couldn't stop thinking about what had happened. "Skeeter's supposed to be my friend! How could he be such a . . . a . . . not friend!"

He wondered how Quailman would handle this problem. Once again, his mind flew into another fantasy.

"Silver Skeeter . . . your behavior will not go unpunished." Quailman spoke seriously to his fellow superhero.

"What behavior?" his silver friend asked.

"HA! As if you didn't know! My Quail Powers have detected your

lying ways and uncovered your
secret passion for Super Sport!"

"Now that you know, what are
you going to do about it, Belt-
Head?"

"I don't know. I mean, I *should* unleash all the powers of the Quail against you; I *should* turn your liquid titanium into peat moss, but you are my best titanium friend. You knew how I felt about Super Sport, but you took her from me. Now I've lost both of you and I feel empty and alone. I think I'll just go back to the Thicket of Solitude. I hope you and Super Sport will be very happy."

"Wait!" shouted Silver Skeeter. "You can't leave me like that! You're right, you *are* my best friend! Please stay! Oh, no . . . can't think . . . very confused . . . feeling helpless and stupefied!"

As soon as Doug awoke from his daydream, he knew what had to be done. "I've got to tell Skeeter that I know what's been happening and let the chips hit the fan. That's the only way."

CHAPTER EIGHT

"I've got to face him sooner or later. I just wish it was later." Doug looked back at his "friends" dancing together. "A lot later."

"Okay, dancers!" Ms. Mimi called as she clapped her hands, gathering everyone's attention. "Let's take our places for the finale, 'Avocado Da Beeta, Baby,' and we will then go home. Ready? One, two, three, and . . ."

The music bellowed below as Doug busily worked the spotlight. There were so many lighting cues for this number that he didn't have time to think about what he was about to do.

"Bravo, bravo!" cheered Ms. Mimi. "Excellent work, my little beets! I'll see you all tomorrow night." And with that she dismissed everyone.

"Hey, Doug," said Skunky, "you wanna go get a root beer and watch my lava lamp for a while? It's torqin'."

"Ah . . . no, thanks, Skunky. There's something I've got to do. Thanks anyhow." Doug dragged himself backstage to talk to Skeeter. As Doug stepped out from behind the prop table, he saw them. Patti and Skeeter— the greatest girl in the world and the biggest backstabber in Bluffington. As he tried to sum- mon up the courage to walk over to them, it happened! Patti put her hand on Skeeter's shoulder and whispered in his ear! Had Skeeter actually won Patti over? As the two of them stood there laughing together, Doug broke out in a cold sweat, his knees

began to knock, and his throat
was so dry he could hardly swal-
low. I can't go through with it!
Doug thought. I've got to get out
of here before they see me.

As he turned to leave, Moo
Sleech placed a toolbox down
behind him. Doug, in the dark-
ness backstage, tripped over the
toolbox, and he fell onto the
costume table. Doug and all the
costumes landed on the floor
together with a thud.

Skeeter and Patti ran to see
what had happened. There, at the
bottom of the pile lay Doug, fran-
tically trying to disguise himself
as an avocado.

"Doug?" Patti asked. "Is that you?"

"Oh, ah . . . hi there, Patti. I didn't see you there," Doug stammered, his head caught in the armhole of the avocado suit.

"What are you doing, man?" asked Skeeter.

"Oh, well, I just thought I'd tell you both that I'm well . . . happy for you two. I mean . . . I guess the best man won . . . I mean, it was just one of those things . . ."

"What are you talking about, Doug?" said Patti, who was very confused.

"Patti Mayonnaise!" Judy shouted. "Your dad's here to pick you up."

"Oh, I've gotta go. See you later, Doug. I hope you're all right. See ya, Skeeter."

"Doug, are you okay, man? You aren't making any sense. Maybe that avocado suit is cutting off the circulation to your brain or something," Skeeter said, trying to help Doug get out of the costume.

"No, Skeet," Doug said, finally removing his head. "I know what I'm talking about. I saw everything. I know about you and Patti."

"Huh? What are you talking about, Doug?"

"I saw you and Patti holding hands at Lucky Duck Park. And I saw her whispering in your ear just a minute ago. I know what's going on . . . I'm not blind, you know."

"You mean you think that Patti and me . . . me and Patti? . . . Ha–ha!" Skeeter laughed.

"Well, why else would you suddenly have a pet hog and a sick toe? You two were meeting secretly in the park . . . and . . . I thought you were my friend, Skeeter."

"I *am* your friend, Doug. Didn't you see Patti's hand?" Skeeter asked.

"Why?"

"We weren't holding hands, Doug. We were practicing our dance numbers. I tripped and knocked her over. She cut her hand. I was helping her put a

Band-Aid on it. We skateboard
guys always carry extra Band-
Aids, you know. Especially if you
wreck a lot, like me."

"Why didn't you tell me? Why
were you sneaking around?"

"I know this sounds silly, but I've been really worried about this dancin' stuff, Doug. I'm not very good and Patti said she'd help me practice. I didn't want anybody to see how bad I am. It's kinda embarrassing, ya know. I just didn't want anybody to find out where we were or what we were doing. I think I do better when nobody else is watching."

"Aw, Skeet," Doug said sheepishly. "I'm sorry. I should have known you could never betray me. Some best friend I am!"

"No problem, man! I mean, I *have* been acting a little weird.

Friends?" Skeeter said, holding up his hand.

"Yes sir!" Doug smiled and slapped Skeeter's hand.

"Let's make a deal."

"What, Skeet?"

"No matter what, no girl will ever come between us, right?"

"Right!" Doug agreed. "Let's go to Swirly's!"

"Oh, Skeeter!" called a voice in the distance.

"Oh, yeah. I almost forgot." Skeeter said, rolling his eyes. "I promised Beebe I'd fix her computer. Let's start this no girls thing tomorrow, okay? See ya, honk, honk!" Skeeter trotted off behind Beebe.

Doug just smiled. Skeet was back!

EPILOGUE

Dear Journal,

The opening night of *A Tale of Two Salads* was a big hit! Of course, there were a few little mistakes here and there. Like when Skeeter tripped and knocked over that whole pitcher of salad dressing into the audience. But, all in all, the show

went pretty well. It was
fun to see Patti and
Skeeter together on
stage. Two of my
favorite people in the

spotlight! I still can't believe I ever suspected Skeeter would betray me. I guess sometimes the thing you are afraid of isn't as bad as you thought it was.

Doug closed his journal and said, "You know, Porkchop, I was so jealous that I almost messed up big-time. I guess when you come right down to it, friends are worth fighting for. And sometimes the person you end up fighting is the one in the mirror. I guess Skeeter's just about the best friend a guy could have."

Porkchop moaned his disapproval. Doug corrected himself quickly, "The best human friend, that is!"